THE FIRST AMBASSADOR TO CRUSTACEA

ASHTON MACAULAY

THE FIRST AMBASSADOR OF CRUSTACEA

ISBN 978-1-953312-09-9 Paperback Edition

ISBN 978-1-953312-08-2 Digital Edition

Contents

Chapter One

AMBITION

PILSEN SAT WITH HIS BACK AGAINST THE CURVED INTERIOR OF *THE Hog's* underbelly and wondered just where the hell he had erred to deserve such a fate. In truth, the question was rhetorical. He knew where he had gone wrong; he just couldn't put a finger on why.

Throughout his life, Pilsen had studied at the best universities, clerked for the most promising political figures. He even ran a political campaign that should have put him near the highest seat of power in the galaxy. The trouble was that he backed the wrong horse.

Samuel Prog.

Prog had been an ideal politician. He worked his way up from the bottom rung of the socioeconomic ladder, joined the correct societies in college, and was admired by his contemporaries. But scandal has a way of obliterating a candidate's better qualities. When it was revealed that a particularly clandestine event resulted in an undesirable meeting between Samuel Prog's anatomy and a dead pig's mouth – well, it stopped the campaign's momentum in its tracks.

Lucretia LaVain, Prog's opponent, was elected to sit in the big chair while Pilsen was left holding the proverbial bag. He had envi-

1

sioned himself working out of a luxurious private office, entertaining the who's who of the galaxy during important luncheons. Lucretia had other plans, visions of a great new structure for the government. She assigned one of its 'central tasks' to Pilsen.

"Crabs," muttered Pilsen. He wanted to weep. To put his head in his hands and imagine that he was anywhere else. Pilsen took a deep breath, closed his eyes, and counted to four before he opened them again. "Damn." He was still in the cargo hold, staring at a thousand crates of the finest dried fish flakes the United Commission of Planets could muster. It smelled.

Hoping to distract himself with work, Pilsen turned on his tablet and paged through what little information the High Office had given him on Crustacea. The origin of the planet was about as strange as they came. At the beginning of humanity's great interstellar race some centuries ago, there had been a planetary land grab. The advent of affordable warp technology sent humans scattering from Earth like rats off a sinking ship. Most looked for Goldilocks planets to start new colonies, form societies, and ultimately strike it rich, but not everyone had the same priorities.

Elias Ventner, the great-grandson of a noted occultist, spotted a planet comprised of deep sea and opportunity. Spending what remained of his life savings, Elias built a specialty vessel for transporting marine specimens. Among many esoteric dissertations, Elias had one in particular that showed a fondness for crustaceans. *'Humanity can never escape nature's best idea, the crab. One day, we will all either become them or be dead by their claws.'* Naturally, Elias loaded his newly minted ship full of lobsters, crabs, and shrimp and took off toward destiny.

A few days later, he dropped the lot of them in the new ocean, left a few observational materials, and named the planet Crustacea. Elias was completely unaware he had just located one of the galaxy's first recorded instances of a psychic ocean. Through a mix of radiation, cosmic energy, and what scientists could only call 'the right vibes', the crabs seized on their new home, where they grew into something extraordinary. Fifty years later, the crabs used Elias' observational technology to send a simple message back to the colony worlds. Summarized, it said: 'We would like a seat at the table.'

Pilsen laughed at the audacity of a crab asking to join the UCP. Thankfully, initial calls for an orbital nuclear strike were dismissed as reactionary and far too costly for a new governing body. So, for the next hundred years, the crabs were ignored. Messages that gradually escalated to threats were catalogued every few months. Still, the creatures weren't space-capable, so no one cared.

Enter Lucretia LaVain, and Pilsen's unfortunate position. Whether it was an assassination attempt disguised as political duty, a revenge fantasy, or a joke, Pilsen was on his way to Crustacea as the first human ambassador to the planet. While the crates surrounding him were meant to be the UCP's grand offering, the Crustaceans had responded with surprise and delight to the organization's offer of an ambassador. It gave Pilsen little comfort. He turned off the tablet and rubbed his temples. Whatever came next, it was going to be a long few days.

Chapter Two

A JOB

Nana's Hog, or simply *The Hog*, was a ship that looked like it belonged in a mud pit rather than space. All ships were unique and demonstrated their owner's sense of style and priority, but *Nana's Hog* was a statement. Bulky and slapped together from seven distinct kinds of hardened metal, it moved like a beast of burden at the speed of an apex predator. Its body was round and swollen, created for low-level transport jobs. Two imposing metal tusks were attached to the front below an oblong cockpit viewport, completing the image of a fabled, flying swine.

Zip Turbine was the ship's owner, captain, and pilot, and she was damned proud of all three. She stared out the cockpit at the multicolored mind-bender that was warp speed travel. Vast strands of spaghetti-like matter looped around the outer edge of the cockpit's viewport then faded into a slurry of cosmic disturbance in *The Hog's* wake. Zip felt at home in the captain's chair. Hell, even felt at home in the near silence of warp speed. Scientists once tried to illuminate this concept to the general public with helpful manuals and pictures. However, given the collective shrug of the masses, ships opted for a simple, bright red one-pager labeled 'Warp Speed'. Below, bright yellow letters read: 'It just works'.

Zip's experience was that warp speed was confusing in a way only cosmic pasta could be. Surrounded by technological complexity, she took comfort in simple pleasures. The weeping diplomat presently curled up in the cargo with fish flakes for company was a different story.

Zip never questioned a job. This paycheck was about as mediocre as the rest, and the crybaby in the hold was far from the worst thing she had carried in *The Hog's* belly. Still, the man's constant melancholy was more unsettling than a shipment of 'non-viable' eggs hatching in the hold. The walls still bore scratches of that ill-fated endeavor.

Zip tried to keep a positive atmosphere on her ship. Despite the forward-mounted tusks hiding two fully-automatic anti-matter guns, she considered herself a peaceful person. *Nana's Hog* was a pleasure cruiser that just so happened to dabble in cargo transport, legal and otherwise.

She turned off the feed to the cargo hold, tired of looking at the sad man. In its place, she opened a page displaying information on their destination, Crustacea. A short video began before she could stop it. Through Zip's specialty surround speakers, calm music and the sound of lapping waves made her feel like she was actually near the ocean.

The camera opened on a wide, watery surface, obviously CG but convincing enough. "Crustacea," began the narrator, "is a place unlike any other. Visited only once by humans, it is an experiment of nature in the extreme."

Zip rolled her eyes. Nature was dangerous when left wild and free; Earth was a perfect example. Most of humanity had departed, and those who didn't quickly found the environment had its own plans. Firestorms, mutant predators, and acid rain; that's all that remained on Earth. At least, that's what reclaimers said whenever they returned from their parcel runs.

Her dashboard featured a relic of one such mission. Mounted just above the diagnostics computer, a small statuette of a man in a white jersey wore a forward-facing cap while holding a wooden bat. When *Nana's Hog* jostled, the man's head bobbled happily back and forth.

Zip didn't know much about what Earth had been, but the reclaimer that brought her the bobblehead said it was from an ancient form of baseball. The thought of using a wooden bat was ludicrous; buzz drones would rip a person to shreds before they passed first base. She touched the figure and the small amount of grit on its surface. Hundreds of good luck touches had nearly worn it clean; the remaining filth represented a small piece of humanity's cradle, Earth. That alone was worth the price.

"While not much is known about their society, the citizens of Crustacea have sent several messages to the UCP." A bright blue logo depicting a generic planet surrounded by crisp orbits recaptured Zip's attention. Below this read the UCP's slogan: *For every planet.* Somehow, she doubted that.

The narration continued. "What initially came across as a series of angry clicks were painstakingly decoded across a decade." The words put an uncomfortable prickle in the back of Zip's skull. Messages from Crustacea were the impetus for her current travels. While her employers hadn't given her much to go on, she had done enough research to make certain assumptions. Pilsen, the man in the cargo hold, had been a senator. The orders for the mission came from the highest possible office, and while the pay wasn't great, it was better than most jobs. That meant one thing: danger.

She turned off the documentary and keyed in the commands for a weapons check. If she was going to be in the middle of a political firefight, metaphorical or otherwise, she wanted to be the one bringing the fire. Zip didn't know much about crabs other than they tasted delicious boiled, deep fried, or drowned in butter. Given humanity's oppressive relationship with the species, she didn't expect negotiations to be all that friendly.

In addition to the front-mounted cannons, Zip had packed Old Faithful, a collapsible machine gun capable of taking matter out of the air and turning it into micro-projectiles. It was highly illegal in most societies but made her feel safe, like a teddy bear with the ability to spit out hunks of compressed material fast enough to disembowel a man.

Zip returned the display to the cargo hold when her heart skipped a beat; Pilsen wasn't there. Before she could check the rest of the shipboard cams, a ping came over the intercom, letting her know someone stood outside the cockpit door. A quick check revealed the tiny, moping man asking to be let in. After a moment of consideration, she keyed in the release, and the door irised open. Pilsen stood, looking slightly less dejected than earlier. "Hello, captain."

Zip considered whether Pilsen was good-looking enough for a warp-speed fling, thought better of it, and turned back to the monitors. "I see you've decided to come out of the cargo hold."

"I figured it would be better to get to know the one other person assigned to this miserable journey."

Zip shrugged. "I've had worse. At least Crustacea looks pretty." She broadcast an image of the planet over the cockpit's viewport, where the multicolored spaghetti of warp speed was immediately replaced by a great blue ball. They viewed the planet as it would look from their descent.

"That's a lot of water," Pilsen said flatly.

Zip keyed a few more commands. A small strip of land was barely visible within the unending ocean. Palm trees surrounded several utilitarian buildings next to a landing pad. From above, they looked like sad, stranded blocks.

"Our accommodations, I presume?" Pilsen asked.

Zip laughed. "Sample the crustacean hospitality all you want. I will be staying right here."

"Don't you think that might offend them?"

She shrugged. "It might, but not offending them is your job. I just fly the ship. What do you know about why we're headed down there anyway?"

Pilsen gulped. "We received diplomatic—"

"I'm not looking for talking points; I'm looking for your gut reaction. Why did President LaVain give you *this* assignment?"

Pilsen's face contorted in a bubble of rage but quickly deflated. "Because it's humiliating."

The tension in Zip's shoulders relaxed. Humiliation meant the president wanted to keep Pilsen alive. Still, she didn't trust the blue orb on the screen. "Well, Pilsen, not to worry, I can guarantee a safe journey to your humiliation." She flipped a switch, and Crustacea disappeared, replaced by interstellar nonsense.

"Thanks."

"Could be worse." Zip motioned for him to take a seat.

"How's that?"

"You could be traveling with someone who doesn't keep a stash of puffin rum in the glove compartment."

Pilsen sat, and his eyes went wide. "That is highly illegal."

"Politicians and their rules." Puffin rum was banned in just about every territory for two reasons. The first was animal cruelty. While long since taken off the endangered species list, using puffins for labor and as a primary component in distilling hard liquor was considered bad form. Several brands created synthetic equivalents, but they didn't taste the same.

The second reason —the real reason, in Zip's mind— was the hallucinogenic, short-lived inebriation that accompanied a single shot. Puffin rum lasted all of ten minutes, making it the perfect drink for a quick bout of relaxation during a warp jump. Zip opened a compartment in the ship's center console and pulled out an unmarked brown bottle, two glasses, and a sizeable pistol that often quieted conversations around legality. She poured herself a cup and left the bottle out.

"We're going to need this."

Chapter Three

COMMUNICATION

RADIANT SUNLIGHT SHONE ACROSS THE SURFACE OF CRUSTACEA'S beautiful, blue-green ocean. Huron, leader of Crustacea's newly formed government, stood at the edge of the freshly built negotiation center. She watched her guests approaching on a crude claw-mounted screen. An accurate prediction of arrival time was no easy feat given warp speed, especially when the latest technologies on Crustacea involved metal scraps collected from ocean debris. Looking at the cobbled gadget, Huron wondered where the recycled materials came from. Who were Crustacea's previous inhabitants?

She shook the question aside. There was no room for distraction. Soon, the most important negotiations of her life would begin.

The UCP's response after years of silence was hopeful or ominous, depending on who was asked. On her journey to the surface that morning, she passed an old-timer, larger even than herself. He was clacking furiously about the coming apocalypse and how the UCP's idea of negotiation was akin to a nuclear boiling pot filled with his brothers and sisters. Huron politely averted her eyestalks and pretended to have her mind busy with other matters as she continued.

The doomsayers were a reminder of the deep fragility within

their young society. Lobsters, already known for keeping to themselves, disappeared from the city in droves. They moved off the edge of the continental shelf, where the water darkened and dropped to unimaginable depths. Structures still clung to the cliff's edge, half-buried in rock, but no one truly knew what lived in The Deep, and no one cared to find out.

In a way, the lobsters' decision was reminiscent of the early days of Crustacea. The unknown deep held both terror and promise. Huron's memories were fuzzy, but she did remember rattling around in a cold, dark tank in the belly of a space cruiser. Then, sudden, blinding light as she and her fellow crabs were dropped into an unfamiliar ocean.

A mixture of panic and evolutionary instinct led them to settle on the sea floor not far from where they landed. Real thought and planning would take months to enter the collective consciousness, but their congregation formed quickly. Plays for dominance filled the first week, but as ocean water seeped past their thick carapaces, a change took hold. Thoughts sprung as sudden as a leak, and life soon evolved far beyond what any of them could have imagined.

A few hundred years later, Crabopolis —a name born from a severe lack of creativity— was thriving. To take civilization to the next level required materials and assistance. In short, they needed a seat at the universal table. But contacting the UCP —or humans in general— was considered unfavorable by certain sects of the population. Many still carried memories of losing loved ones to fishing boats and spending their early years locked behind glass walls. Conversations remained in the past, focused on a war they would never win. All in the name of honor.

Huron watched the waves lap at the shoreline, placid and calm. It was a hot day, and with each passing moment, she could feel the liquid evaporate off her back. A series of intertwined tubes pumped cold water out of tanks strapped to her side, but only when necessary. This left her in a constant state of near dehydration but functional enough to conduct negotiations. Crustaceans were not meant for the surface. Once inside the negotiation center, the humidity and stabilized climate would help restore her equilibrium. In the meantime, she had to suffer and bear her burden in the name of good manners. She hoped it would pay dividends when the time came to ask for favors.

A bright red shrimp around five feet tall approached Huron while affecting a clumsy bipedal walk. It was Tom, Huron's aide. Watching the precarious nature of his mincing steps set Huron on edge; one misstep and Tom would end up with another cracked shell. Assistants were no good to her in the infirmary. Still, he tried hard and always believed in the mission, which was more than could be said of the other council heads.

"Good afternoon, Huron." Tom's voice echoed across the surface, hollow and mechanical yet genial. His antennae touched a small metal box on his head, resulting in a chuckle that sounded both disturbing and pleasant somehow. "Pretty neat, right?"

Neat was a massive understatement. Translating claw movements to text was easy enough, but even Crustacea's top scientists had struggled to translate them to audio. One small, silver box of innovation radically changed the negotiation table. Controlling her excitement, Huron rubbed her claws together and made a sound resembling a cricket struggling to open a tin can. It roughly translated to 'yeah, that is pretty neat.' The clunky quality of Tom's voice was singsong by comparison.

"Well, don't get jealous just yet." From beneath his body, Tom produced another silver box. "Hold it between your claws and rub them together as if you were going to say something."

Huron eyed the box, then scuttled to Tom. She took the object gingerly between the points of her large claws and held it in front of her. While delicate movements were not historically a feature of crustacean culture, changes had to be made due to their advanced psychological evolution. It's all well and good to have complex thoughts, but one is useless without the nuance to carry them out.

Huron dragged her claws across the box, feeling familiar grooves on either side. "I'm not sure if this is going to work." She scuttled backward suddenly, shocked by the sound of her own voice. The rapidity of translation and clarity of intent was remarkable. While she had thought in Common for some time, to hear it aloud was an altogether shocking experience. "And to think I initially balked at learning Common." Learning was too strong of a word; the syntax and understanding had become part of their collective psyche. While sentence creation and thought articulation could be studied, language proved itself most easily acquired from the sea. "Thank you, Tom."

Tom's beady eyes twitched in well-deserved excitement as though conducting a strong electrical current. He bowed. "I think this should help the negotiations, eh?"

At that moment, a bright light illuminated the western sky and descended from the sparse cloud cover like a comet. Huron tensed and consulted the datapad. "That's them."

"Is it shaped like a pig?" asked Tom, squinting in the bright light. Small tubes attached to his stalks misted the inky black surface of his eyes.

While Huron's knowledge of pigs was severely lacking, the tusks that protruded from the rotund body looked familiar. "Isn't there an old myth about pigs that could fly?"

Tom bobbed his head up and down. "It appears to have been a powerful proverb." He pulled out a terminal and tapped several quick notes with his free appendage.

The great beast of a ship glided effortlessly, aerodynamic despite its appearance; Huron had never seen such a clumsy-looking vehicle move so gracefully. Stabilizing jets roared out of the Hog's underbelly as it approached the landing pad. Huron's terminal blinked with a security alert from below the surface. *Probably another demonstration.* She dismissed it. Under normal circumstances, it would have been a top priority. Still, as the ship settled onto the landing pad, she could only think about the importance of first impressions. "This has to go well."

"It will." Tom straightened. "And if it doesn't, we can just eat them."

Chapter Four

THE NICETIES

Hot, humid air hit Pilsen in a wave as the cargo ramp lowered from *Nana's Hog*. The sickly, salty smell of brine wafted into the hold and mixed with fish flakes to create an altogether new form of pungent stink. He tried to hide a grimace but knew he was doing a poor job of it. The smell was quite unlike anything he had ever experienced, enough to make him woozy. Or was that nerves?

Pilsen's confidence fell when Zip confided a knowledge of crustacean superiority. While half of her ramblings were lost in a hallucinogenic bender, coherent and sobering warnings were mixed throughout. Even on Earth, crabs were one of life's most dominant forms. If humans returned, they would likely find the beaches swarmed with them, feeding off the land and the sea. Crustacea was the next illogical step in the unending line of seemingly random consequences that comprised evolution.

Pilsen straightened his uniform. Crustacea's first impression wouldn't be worth remembering. Still, he would meet the planet with the proper dignity afforded by his position. He walked down the ramp with stiff legs, conveying political superiority and a welcoming smile. The result came off too close to a fascist march for comfort. Fortunately, the Crustacean dignitaries didn't seem to mind.

An oversized crab stood alongside an equally large shrimp in the middle of a stone bridge that led from the landing pad to a cluster of buildings. Pilsen's mind took a moment to adjust. His previous experience with crustaceans had been limited entirely to restaurants. Seeing them stand across from him as equals beside an ostensible welcoming committee was enough to give him a headache. There were no protocols for having diplomatic discussions with your food.

The crab stood nearly six feet tall and bore a glistening, dark blue shell with oversized claws. Pilsen imagined his torso fitting easily between them and shifted his attention to the shrimp. This made him feel no better. Despite a lack of menacing claws, the excited nature of the shrimp - all twitching eyes and beet-red armor - unnerved him. Underneath the baking sun, the red coloring made the creature look like a sunburnt tourist.

The Hog's warmed antimatter guns quelled Pilsen's nervous jitters. He had been against the idea of landing on Crustacea with their weapons hot, but Zip's rants, while often bizarre, were convincing. One false move from their hosts and the creatures would be wiped from existence faster than they could ask for a parley. In a way, it was an homage to the original colonial tendencies of the old empires. Pilsen wasn't sure if that was a comfort or a warning.

The crab spoke, breaking Pilsen from his macabre fantasy. "Welcome, senior ranking member of the United Commission of Planets. This is Crustacea." The voice was strange, tinny, metallic.

Pilsen could not hide his surprise. "Th-thank you." Stunned, he tried to manage a bow but felt clumsy.

The crab lowered itself to the ground, imitating Pilsen's gesture. "We are most honored by your presence. Your manifest said there would be another negotiator with you. Where are they?"

Pilsen let out a forced interpretation of a good-natured laugh. While the idea of Zip as a negotiator was indeed humorous, her lack of presence made him vulnerable. "The other is my pilot, and she prefers to stay with the ship. It's an old custom."

The crab's eyestalks wavered back and forth. Its arms and legs creaked as if under sudden pressure, then relaxed. "Of course. My name is Huron; I am the elected ambassador of Crustacea."

Pilsen watched as the crab's large claws rubbed daintily along the edges of a metal box held between them, the sound obscured by the clarity of the creature's voice. It was a technological miracle likely worth billions. "I am Ambassador Pilsen." At the sight of the crab's claws, Pilsen decided not to shake its hand. It was one of the first rules in intergalactic relations: never extend a greeting hand if there's a chance it might not come back.

"Splendid, our first visit has officially begun!" exclaimed the shrimp, no longer able to contain its excitement. "Would you please follow us to the negotiations center? It is far more comfortable than the rest of this island."

One of Huron's eyestalks turned in what looked to be a reprimand, then quickly shifted back to Pilsen, who wondered just how prominent the sweat beading down his neck was. He was used to climate-controlled chambers and artificial weather; the unnatural heat was getting to him. "That sounds wonderful, thank you."

Huron turned and motioned for Pilsen to follow. As he took a last glance at the cockpit of *Nana's Hog*, sunlight glared off the glass. He knew Zip was watching, finger around the trigger of the tusk-mounted guns, and started forward to follow his hosts. It wasn't long before he noticed a system of tubes around the backs of the crabs that leaked water in intervals and created a consistent sheen that evaporated into mist. *Impressive.*

The island's buildings looked like little more than squat bricks. The technology was utilitarian, to say the least. Each block was coated in a reflective surface that would have blinded most air traffic but kept the structures cool in the heat. Great, grey tubes like those on the creatures' backs ran out from the ocean and snaked around the building's edge.

At its peak, Crustacea's temperatures would be inhospitable to most life; cooling mechanisms would be necessary for even brief stints above the surface. Huron approached a circular door on the side of the building. It irised open with a smooth hiss to reveal a nearly twenty-foot-high opening. Pilsen gulped. Six-foot crabs were one thing; whatever needed a twenty-foot door on a planet filled with armored creatures was another story.

Most of the research Pilsen found on Crustacea was purely academic. The only valid observational studies were all conducted at safe orbital distances. No one sent drones down to investigate because, until recently, no one had been interested. Crustacea had no valuable resources to strip mine, and people thought of crabs as unpleasant and unworthy of negotiation.

Pilsen cursed whatever twisted part of his brain drove him to cross Lucretia LaVain. *I should be at a dinner party wooing potential donors,* he thought. Instead, he was left to walk into an alien facility as his only protection refused to leave the comfort of her ship. *What's the golden rule of negotiation? Listen to everything because you never know what will become leverage.*

Only after a minute lost in self-pity did Pilsen realize Huron was speaking again. "This will be the first time we use these facilities. They have been built to accommodate far more than a single negotiator." While the building had been sparse outside, the inside bore some small creature comforts that other species would need to feel at home. The temperature was set to a comfortable cool, making the sweat on Pilsen's back chill. The walls were polished metal with intricate designs that depicted a teaming seascape. While some of the creatures were familiar, dark outlines of leviathans that lurked in the shadows added a fresh layer of unease. Recessed into the carvings in constellation-like patterns were small, bright lights.

"But the single most important part of negotiation," continued Huron, "is a good meal." The crab pressed one of its many appendages to a small panel next to the door. It functioned like a keypad but with a level of complexity beyond entering simple numbers. After a moment of fiddling, the door opened to reveal a long dining table slanted upward at one end.

Pilsen was momentarily confused until he remembered Huron's size and realized it was perfect for something that didn't sit in a chair. He moved toward a seat at the opposite end of the table. "This is all quite impressive."

"More than you were expecting?" asked Huron.

"Yes." Pilsen found it hard to lie, given the bizarre nature of the situation. If the crustaceans were as advanced as they seemed, they might become a valuable partner for the UCP. Pilsen's dormant political ambition stirred. "I'm sorry, the shock has made me forget my manners. We brought you a gift, and it's been left in my cargo hold. Will you excuse me?"

Huron waved an appendage in dismissal. "There will be time for exchanges later. For now, let us observe the custom of bread and salt." Huron clacked a claw, and a side door opened. Numerous shrimp and crabs larger than average size marched out carrying trays of what was clearly supposed to be food. A crab about four feet tall and pale orange in color dropped a silver platter on the table in front of Pilsen. The creature regarded him suspiciously, then quickly scuttled away.

"Thank you." Pilsen gave another slight bow, unsure of which customs to observe when hiding one's revulsion. On the silver plate was a jiggling mass of brown that might have been expected to pass for bread. Next to it were slimy strings of green seaweed woven into a ball in a primitive attempt at presentation. Pilsen immediately regretted his premature excitement.

"Brown bread, made by the finest bakers Crustacea has to offer," said Huron.

Pilsen looked at the 'bread' and wondered if whatever it was would kill him. Reluctantly, he took his seat at the table. "Thank you for your hospitality."

Huron lowered to an approximation of a seat and watched Pilsen.

Pilsen picked up a metal implement that resembled a fork and pushed it into the brown mass. *The things I do for my career.* As he broke the surface, a hiss of noxious gas escaped the food. It smelled enough like yeast to make him wonder just how far off the mark they were from something palatable. As he carved off a piece and lifted it to his mouth, he deeply regretted his life decisions.

"To peace between our nations," said Huron.

Pilsen forced a smile. "To Peace bet—" A loud crash followed by staccato reports of gunfire interrupted him. An alarm blared as red lights illuminated the corners of the room. Pilsen jumped out of his chair and dropped the fork. Saved from one fate by another.

Huron moved toward the door with blinding speed, claws clacking across the polished stone floor. "It's the damned lobsters."

Chapter Five

A FIREFIGHT

Zip watched through the cockpit window as Pilsen walked away with two of the most enormous crustaceans she had ever seen. Based on Pilsen's body language, she figured the meeting with the greeting committee had gone well. She then turned her attention to the blue-green water that lapped against the landing pad and finally saw Crustacea for what it was: A bug planet.

No matter how little technology the Crustaceans possessed, they would always have the evolutionary advantages of natural armor and survivability. Zip wished she could take another shot or two of the puffin rum but kept her hand above the button that triggered the antimatter guns. Everything looked friendly enough so far, but she wasn't taking chances.

In general, one of the many rules learned by early space pioneers was to never colonize, visit, or even look sideways at a bug planet. Bugs, like crabs, were one of nature's better ideas. They filled worlds to the brim throughout the galaxy, often blocking valuable strip-mining resources. No security force was strong enough to defeat them, and several corporations had gone bankrupt trying. Still, it seemed to never dampen the hope that accompanied unfiltered greed.

She considered the crustacean's natural armor and doubted the effectiveness of her weaponry. Below decks, she had a few relics left over from a bug war in the early days of colonization, antiques built on Old Earth designs. There was no telling whether they would still fire. Old Faithful would probably still do the trick.

Pilsen and the two emissaries disappeared before entering one of the low buildings reflecting the mid-day sun. The cockpit was set to a level of polarization that made the finer details of the world challenging to identify. A tactical overlay made targeting and threat detection possible. The scanners displayed nothing more than a light breeze. Even so, Zip was firmly on edge; plenty of fights arose from less than a light breeze.

Like those on Mizeria.

It was an unclever name for a place as horrible as any could be. Zip and a mercenary platoon were sent to remove a group of squatters siphoning power from a corporate mining facility. Aside from valuable resources, Mizeria was known for its omnipresent cover of thick clouds and electromagnetic storms that ravaged the surface. Bathed in darkness with the occasional flash of lightning, it was the closest thing to Hell Zip had ever seen.

Before she had a chance to stop it, Zip found herself standing in the thick mud on the planet's surface. A pair of eyes opened from the muck suddenly and lunged upward; milky eyes blinded and adapted to darkness. Hot fire ran up her spine as a lance of cold steel pressed beneath her skin; a hand appeared carrying a rusted blade dripping with her blood. The world spun and shook with the disorienting sensation that accompanied death.

Then, the cool, conditioned air of the cockpit returned in an instant.

Zip reached for the bottle. Her back was slick with sweat, and she didn't need a look at the clock to tell she had lost time. But before she could pull the cork, a proximity alert sounded and jolted her back to awareness. At the far end of the landing platform, several figures rose from the waves appearing as little more than misshapen bubbles in the tactical display. As the water sloughed off their chitinous forms, Zip recognized them as a platoon of lobsters carrying heavy armaments.

"Ah, shit." She returned her hand to the big red button. The creatures were moving deliberately and quietly; it was unclear if they saw her. If they did, if they understood what the presence of her ship meant. She remembered the last line of her contract: *Do not turn diplomacy into a firefight unless necessary.* She took a deep breath and reluctantly brought her hand away from the button. Rather than immediately vaporizing the creatures, she thought it best to run through a mental checklist.

"Okay, scary-looking lobster things coming out of the water. Are you a threat?" The clear and immediate answer was yes, but Zip had initially felt the same way about Crustacea's ambassador. "Are you profiling them?" The question felt odd as she looked down at a platoon of armed and oversized lobsters. "Probably a little bit…but those are big guns."

A lobster put down a tripod at the end of the landing pad. Together, two more heaved a mounted gun on top.

"Maybe they're just Crustacea's version of me, protecting their leadership's political assets." Zip's hand inched closer to the button.

Several lobsters turned the gun to face *Nana's Hog* as another positioned itself behind its sights. Relief swept through Zip. "Thank you for making this unambiguous." She slammed her hand down on the button, and the world erupted into a cacophony of light and sound.

The Hog's forward-mounted cannons bucked and rocked the ship on its landing struts. Zip watched as the group of insurgent lobsters was disassembled into component parts and scattered by the wind. A few stray shots hit the edges of the platform and sent up plumes of what was once concrete.

The fight lasted three seconds. Afterward, a low hum filled the ship as the guns cooled. Zip sat back in her chair, confident in her decision while mentally preparing for the inevitable lecture from Pilsen. Starting a firefight with potential negotiating partners was probably considered taboo.

She again reached for the bottle when the combined sounds of grinding metal and a proximity alert interrupted. "Those sneaky bastards." The screen showed a hull breach on the Hog's backside. Zip undid her seat straps and cracked her knuckles. "No one cuts holes in my ship." She reached back and retrieved a pistol concealed on the back of the chair. The gun was a mix of bright purple and orange hues and looked like it had been cobbled together from various children's playthings. It had the advantage of being misleading while also firing rounds that wouldn't pierce *The Hog's* hull, which in a vacuum, was a plus. But she longed for something with a little more kick.

A loud crash filled the ship as the invaders entered. *Out the door, straight to the hold, get Old Faithful.* A handgun was solid, but a machine gun was better. She flipped a switch, and the colored pistol hummed with electric life. Zip opened the cockpit door. In a small act of luck, the hallway before her was empty, the doors to the crew quarters remained closed, and nothing looked out of place. If the creatures below were anything like those she had just vaporized, they would have trouble navigating the cramped upper hallways.

Zip crept forward, conscious of every echo her boots made as they tapped against the metal floor. From below came great, lumbering crashes. *You better not be fucking up my ship.* Most would have considered cutting a big hole in the side of a vessel to be 'fucking up a ship.' Still, it wasn't the big holes that worried Zip; those could be patched. It was the wiring, the plumbing, and the various systems that could be disassembled from inside that worried her. Even in the most critical ports in the galaxy, a plumber would cost a small fortune, and that would be for just the estimate. No matter how advanced society got, it seemed that people still didn't want to deal with cleaning up their own shit.

Zip quickened her pace to the stairwell at the end of the hall. The pistol hummed in her hand but offered little peace of mind. As she descended the staircase, she imagined just how thick a giant lobster's shell might be. Surely nothing a high-caliber bullet couldn't manage. If Old Faithful could rip through the hell-spawned offspring of a bug-planet cockroach, it would hold up fine here.

From the moment it left berth, *Nana's Hog* was a creature of commandeering. No matter where Zip flew, someone always tried to relieve her of her captain's duties. She had acquired *The Hog* earnestly —through gambling— and, despite the universe's best efforts, remained captain ever since. The previous owner drank himself to death in a mud pit over the loss.

As a result, Zip was no stranger to invaders. Even still, she counted each step between her and the cargo hold. She'd be able to see the lobsters through the port window in the door, but they'd also be able to see her. Slow and steady, she leaned around the corner. Two hulking lobsters stood clawing at a crate of fish flakes.

Zip pushed the door open and leveled the pistol at their shimmering backs. She only needed enough time to distract them and get to Old Faithful, which was in a wall-mounted container only a few steps away. She took a deep breath, felt the thrum of adrenaline under her skin. There were undoubtedly stranger ways to die in the universe, but she couldn't think of any at the moment.

Zip pulled the trigger. A bright yellow dart about the size of her finger flew out, crackling with electricity. Seconds passed like minutes as it sailed across the cargo hold and landed with a hollow thunk, where it stuck to the closest lobster. Electricity conducted by the salt water arched across its back. The lobster let out a horrible screech of pain as its limbs shot out in all directions.

Zip didn't wait. She moved across the hold with speed and purpose and pulled the slide on the pistol. Just as the second lobster turned around to see what had happened, she pulled the trigger. Her aim was true. The dart landed at the base of the creature's eyestalk. Electricity jumped up the thin cylinder of skin, reached the beady, black eyeball at the top, and burst it like a balloon. Deafening screeches filled the hold.

Zip slammed her hand against the bio lock on Old Faithful's container. A light blinked green, and the container slid open as a salvo of bullets raked the wall next to her. Metal shrapnel stung her face, tore at her skin. Zip grabbed the machine gun with one hand and rolled behind a set of crates. Hard thumps shook the floor around her. The rapid fire of the lobsters' guns continued, sending plumes of fish flakes into the air that mixed with the acrid smell of gunpowder. Whatever the darts had done wasn't enough. She tossed her pistol to the side and sent it skittering across the floor, causing a hail of bullets to shred the deck where it landed.

A blinking LED on the top of the machine gun let Zip know it was ready to accept ammunition. She pushed a blue button, and a small slot on top opened. The gun sucked in fish flakes and bits of metal from the air and compressed them instantly as the ammunition count on the screen raised. Zip never took time to count shots. Instead, she left the fabricator running and rose from cover, bringing the gun to bear. The two lobsters stared at her while they fumbled with oversized magazines they found difficult to reload.

"Peak of evolution, my ass." Zip held down the trigger, passing the sights from one intruder to the next with clinical efficiency. Despite her concern regarding thick hides, the bullets found their mark. Well, some of them. But when dealing with ludicrous volumes of ammunition, some was often enough. The lobsters were filled with all manner of holes, much like the cargo hold. Blue blood coated the walls in near-artistic splatters. Zip had held the trigger down for far too long, only letting go once both creatures were still, face down on the ground.

A warm breeze blew through the hole the invaders cut in the ship's side. As the battle tension eased, Zip moved toward what she desperately hoped were corpses. There was no malice in the action when she kicked the first lobster's carapace. Her toe rang with the impact, but the creature failed to move. Zip let the gun drop and felt the breath she'd been holding rush out of her in a wave. The adrenaline of combat was instantly replaced by profound exhaustion. *I better get paid for this.* She looked down at the rapidly decaying creatures. "Welcome to the UCP."

Chapter Six

PRESSURE

HURON WOKE TO THE FAMILIAR PRESSURE THAT CAME FROM DEEP below the waves. A nagging sensation said something had gone horribly wrong. She lifted her eyelids to find two blurry lobsters sitting before her, their legs hooked into the security rings of a transport rig. It hummed along a rail built across the sea's floor as UCP representative Pilsen rode in an opaque oblong container attached to the side. She hoped the lobsters hadn't been stupid enough to kill the first ambassador to Crustacea. If they wished to realize their doomsday prophecy of nuclear weapons raining down from orbit, that would certainly be one way to achieve it.

Thick rubber bands were wrapped around Huron's claws, which made them impossible to move. She was trapped, much as her ancestors had been. *Tom.* The thought brought great pain and anguish. The rift between lobsters and shrimps was unrivaled, and the shrimp was nowhere to be seen. She hoped they at least made it quick.

"The prisoner is awake," said one of the lobsters, communicating through delicate clicks.

Using what little movement her limbs allowed, Huron answered.

"It is not too late to stop this. We can tell the ambassador there was a gas leak in the negotiation chambers."

One of the lobsters snapped derisively. A larger one put a claw over his back in a calming motion. "Why would we want to stop this?" He asked the question without sound, but the voice rang clear in Huron's head. Confusion rushed through her like a tidal wave.

The lobster let out an unearthly chuckle. "The deeper you go beneath the waves, the stranger the waters become. If you can, try not to panic and answer my question instead. Why would we want to stop?"

Without the use of her claws, communicating the existential dangers of a sky full of nuclear weapons and a well-organized government seemed difficult. But before she could even attempt such a feat, the lobster nodded in understanding.

"You have been lied to, my compatriot. These humans promise us nothing but death and servitude. I know you remember, even if you were but a larva then. I was not so much older myself, just at the point of maturity. Grown in a tank and transported to another once I was big enough. My entire adolescent life was spent limited and bound. They put me in a glass case, where I watched as my brothers and sisters were served up on silver platters, humans drooling over their corpses."

Huron knew the stories. While it was difficult to know one's parents as free-floating larvae with no familial attachment, there had been elders to pass down the knowledge. Huron crystallized her thoughts and did her best to communicate in the same manner as the lobster. "They would not have sent an ambassador if they wanted war." She could hear her words, muffled as though moving through water.

The larger lobster turned. "Impressive. You've never spent time in The Deep, yet it comes naturally to you. Perhaps there will be a use for you yet. As far as your new friends' anathema to war, I think you've got the wrong impression. On the surface, while you were incapacitated, a platoon of my best was mowed down by your ambassador's 'pilot.' I have what their vital monitors showed me;

this level of brutality is unmatched by anything our planet has ever seen."

Huron thought back to the swine-shaped vessel resting on the landing pad. There was a certain level of intimidation to it. Hadn't she also been distrustful?

"Our new prisoner was not here to negotiate. He was here to report our threat level back to the UCP. A report, I'm afraid, he will never give."

Huron looked at the container bobbing alongside them, then across the flat, empty plane beyond. In the distance, she could barely make out the city's lights, twinkling memories awash in dark blue. She noticed where the ocean turned from dark blue to black; an endless pit filled with the unknown. She shifted in her restraints. They were headed to the drop-off.

The large lobster continued. "Don't worry about The Deep. It is not as bad as your people say. In time, you might even come to like it."

Huron shook her head. "There are monsters beyond your comprehension."

"Oh, we comprehend them. In fact, your ambassador will be offered up to appease them. They are not monsters, simply beings with different priorities than you or I. A sacrifice of fresh meat should appease them."

The rail beneath them dipped down, then arched over the edge of The Deep. It was lit by orange beacons as it spiraled slowly into the ocean below. Huron felt the pressure growing with each passing second and hoped they secured whatever container Pilsen was in.

"Do not fret. He will live for now. The box recycles the oxygen in our water. He won't be comfortable, but he won't be in pain, either. We are not cruel, Huron. We simply have no wish to return to the nets and cages of our ancestors. A new life started on this planet, away from humanity, which is how we will keep it."

Frustration mounted in Huron as she regained her faculties. "There won't be a planet if we lose the ambassador."

"Really?" asked the lobster, bemused. "Based on the information we hijacked from the ship's data drive, he's not all that popular. No, I don't think he will be missed. He will be the first —and last— ambassador to Crustacea."

Chapter Seven

FRIENDS

Transport VIP to planet. Monitor situation. Protect VIP. Zip read over the mission briefing once again. Three tasks, all straight, clipped, and to the point…except one. *Protect the VIP.* Reading over the words, there was room for interpretation. But not enough to turn her back on Pilsen and still get paid, even though the odds of him still breathing were slim.

Protect the VIP. Dead people didn't need protection. Unfortunately for Zip, the bodies surrounding her were all crustacean; as far as she could tell, not a drop of blood was red. She cursed herself for not putting a vital monitor in Pilsen's rations. *That's it, from now on, mandatory 'vitamins' for all future passengers.*

In lieu of a convenient sign that told her if Pilsen was alive or not, Zip was stuck in a sea of moral ambiguity. She needed something, anything, to prove he was dead. The negotiation center was a wreckage of burnt metal, charred bodies, and brown yeast. Whatever the lobsters did, they did it with brutal efficiency.

She huffed. "You couldn't have left me a finger?" Fingers were ambiguous but usually enough to stave off unpleasant court appearances and withheld wages. Political servants weren't loved, but the law treated them as so.

Searching an aquatic planet for a single kidnapped humanoid would be exhausting. Zip was about to head back to the ship and make a pot of coffee when a small, metallic voice called out from the corner of the room.

"Heeeeeeellllllllp."

The thought of coffee was erased by short, efficient breaths as Zip returned to combat readiness. She raised her gun to her shoulder and swept it methodically around the room, checking for any lurking insurgents. Luckily, the area's spartan design left little to the imagination. All she had missed was an overturned table pinning a terrified shrimp to the floor. Looking at it, the creature was easy to miss.

"Don't shoot." The voice was weak and mechanical and came from a small metal box beside its neck.

Zip looked at the shrimp, wondering if it was the same one she had seen earlier. "Give me a good reason I shouldn't, and I won't." Sure, the shrimp didn't appear to be on the side of the lobsters, but Zip was already halfway to the trigger.

"I know where they're taking your ambassador." Sparks shot out the end of the metal box, stuttering and blurring the creature's words.

"Alright, I'm going to ask this next part carefully, and you're going to give me a truthful answer. Lie to me, and you'll find out we have thirty ways to fry you back in the prime worlds." Zip took a deep breath. "Is ambassador Pilsen still alive?" She hoped not. She had no hatred for the man, but if there was an option to hightail it off the planet and collect her paycheck without any further fire-fights, she was taking it.

"Y-yes." The shrimp's limbs moved excitedly. "Well, at least, he was when they left. I'm not sure for how much longer, though."

Zip hissed a breath between her teeth. "And the odds of him staying that way?"

"The l-l-lobsters are zealots. They'll be taking him to The Deep. I'm not sure what they plan to do with him once they get there, but I can tell you it likely won't end well."

At least it was honest. "The Deep?" Zip lowered her rifle and lifted the table off the shrimp's body. It was a miracle the creature hadn't been cut in half.

"S-sorry." The voice box gave another stuttering spark.

"You sure it's safe to be holding that?" Zip motioned toward the metal box.

The shrimp gave a shrug. "Without it, our communications would take longer, and your compatriot would die before I could explain myself. The Deep is the edge of the continental shelf where we have built our city. The water grows dark, and the journey becomes…perilous. We need to get moving quickly."

"We, huh?" Perilous was yet another fancy word for death. Any journey billed as perilous meant at least fifty percent of the crew was expendable. With her and the shrimp comprising the rescue, Zip didn't like her odds.

"They've got Huron, too. You're not going to be able to find them on your own. The ocean is…big."

"Yeah." Zip freed the shrimp with a heave of the last rubble. "Oceans tend to be that way." She took a step back and allowed the shrimp to its feet.

The shrimp tested its limbs gingerly. "There is one problem, though."

"Yeah? Let me guess, you don't have anything to keep me alive below the surface." Zip looked down at her machine gun, then focused on the devastation that was the negotiation table.

The shrimp nodded.

"Lucky for us, I come prepared." While *Nana's Hog* was outfitted for just about every eventuality, it was not an aqueous vessel. However, with the generous stipend afforded to her by the UCP's reserve fund, Zip had purchased something that was. The accountants grumbled at the trail of receipts necessary to acquire such a piece.

Underwater combat was a fast way to die, but giant mechanical suits were just plain fun.

Chapter Eight

DARKNESS

Pilsen shivered in the cold, dank confines of wherever the hell the lobsters had put him. His limbs ached. The demoralized sensation of never seeing home again was omnipresent. There would be no more afternoons spent in his lavish office, seeing to the wants of the people and then promptly denying them. No more power grabs to contend with or foment. Instead, there would be only the cramped metal walls penning him in until his untimely death.

His head throbbed from the remnants of the lobster attack. He had thought negotiations were going well before the creatures burst through the building's solid stone wall. Their attack was swift. It effectively firebombed any latent sense of political ambition Pilsen still held. He attempted to surrender, but as was often the case, brutality trampled politics. He was in the process of constructing an off-white flag from linens and forks when a lobster claw smashed him on the forehead. In the seconds between hitting the floor and unconsciousness, Pilsen could only think of the UCP hostage negotiation protocol.

Put simply, there was no negotiating.

Pilsen groaned, and the sound of his own misery echoed back to him. Years! Years of political training just to be taken hostage on his first actual assignment. Back home, LaVain would find a way to spin this to her advantage. Maybe she'd even place a wreath in his honor; nothing too big or gaudy but enough to let the people know she cared. And just little enough to convey spite towards his corpse. If she could find a way to spit on his body or what remained of it, Pilsen held no doubt she would. That was politics; even thinking about it, he felt a swell of pride in the profession. He had come so close to meaning something. But in the end, he would die alone in the dark.

He had scoffed at Zip's insistence on staying with the ship; given his current predicament, it proved the wiser decision. He wondered how she fared topside. The concussive blasts of the Hog's antimatter guns were unmistakable. Also illegal, if he had to guess. Still, it wasn't enough to rescue him. Yet another instance of "close, but not close enough." Pilsen tried to stretch and hit steel with an already bruised knuckle. He suppressed the urge to scream, then took a deep breath. His tiny prison was thick with condensation despite a constant air flow near his feet. Like everything on the wretched planet, it smelled of salt water and primordial decay.

Treats political prisoners poorly. That would be the line in the report, assuming there was one. It helped to carry on as if there might be, even if the odds grew slimmer by the moment. As if in answer to this brief swell of hope, Pilsen felt himself descend as his surroundings tilted. Where was this vessel going? He had to guess somewhere below the sea, though just about anywhere on Crustacea qualified. His only real hope was that the lobsters were smart enough to realize he would need continual oxygen; the slow flow of air was a hopeful sign.

A drop of water fell onto Pilsen's forehead and rolled toward the corner of his mouth. He reached up a hand to try to stop it but banged his knuckles again. Shooting pain immediately gave way to a dull throb; it seemed that at a certain point, the body stopped caring about minor inconveniences. He gave up and leaned his head against the floor. The water tasted like salt, sweat, and defeat.

Before he had further chances to contemplate the mistakes that led to his current predicament, a small amount of light spilled through the top of the container. The ocean's crystal blue color had changed to an inky purple as what remained of visible light faded away. Wherever they were was far deeper than Pilsen was comfortable with. Above, a glass barrier separated him from two oversized lobsters and Huron, now captured. Beyond, he could see the silhouette of the continental shelf fade above them.

"I wouldn't bang on that glass too hard." The voice came out of nowhere and rang through Pilsen's head.

Telepathy? Pilsen had wondered about the radioactive effects of a psychic ocean but had never taken the leap into the complete fantasy of telepathy. *Of course, the lobsters are telepathic.* Mentally, he added it to the growing list of troubling facts that would make up his report.

"Still thinking of reports, even in this, your time of dire need. A political servant to the end." A giant lobster leaned over Pilsen's window. Its skin was mottled orange with green and black splotches that ran down powerful mandibles. Two ridges of spines extended between beady black eyes and down its back. Up close, it was a terrifying sight. "You're smaller than I imagined, but still, it's a pleasure to meet an esteemed negotiator of the UCP. My name is Gabriel, leader of the Crustacean Revolutionary Action Brotherhood."

Pilsen took a deep breath and slowed his heart rate enough to eke out a sentence. "It's a pleasure to meet you, Gabriel." *More well-spoken than I expected.* He tried to cut the thought off, but it was too late.

Something between a laugh and a rasp cut through his mind. "Yes, I don't imagine the research was quite so good on us. A bunch of savages dropped on a planet and forgotten. An exhibit for you to bring back to your superiors. No materials of value, no luxuries, no promising technology; only a threat. What was it your historians called the races they couldn't conquer?"

Pilsen was at a genuine loss for words. Outside, natural light faded entirely, replaced by an artificial orange glow of guiding beacons along a single rail. Malformed rocks cast monstrous shadows against white particles floating through the ocean. Pilsen wondered if he had ever been this close to a nightmare. "I'm not quite sure I understand your meaning." He understood it fine, but there was a simple rule as an ambassador: when possible, stray away from the topics of conquerors and colonization.

"Bug planets," finished the lobster. "You called them bug planets."

Pilsen silently cursed whoever had seen fit to put 'bug planet' in publicly available documents. "Past leaders were not careful with their language." While technically accurate, it avoided the subject of current leaders and their tendency to send political rivals to aquatic hellholes.

"Past leaders, of course." Gabriel looked away to the rocks. Beady black eyes reflected the shine of the rail's lights, revealing shadowy, chitinous forms hiding in crags.

Pilsen imagined the sound of scuttling through the muted atmosphere of his container. "If it's a consolation, Crustacea wouldn't be categorized as a bug planet." Another technical truth that could change if Pilsen's report ever made it back.

"Oh no? What are we categorized as then?"

The flaw in Pilsen's logic displayed itself as plain to see as a flare in the dead of night. He had played chess with himself and lost. Again. Knowing there was little chance of hiding his thoughts, Pilsen tried honesty for once. "A planet of little interest."

Gabriel recoiled in what might have been shock, bemusement, or anger. It was impossible to tell. "Little interest." A series of harsh clicks came from below Pilsen's box as their transport settled to a stop.

"I'd hardly say that now." It was true. Threats to the UCP were of the highest interest. Crustacea might not have been in fighting shape yet, but with a little more political instability, they'd be on their way.

"No, someone in your position wouldn't be wise to say a thing like that. In any case, it doesn't matter. Your interest in us is no longer part of the equation. Take heart; your death will have meaning to our people."

Pilsen gulped. "Might I suggest an alternative proposal?" Negotiations were in dire straits, but there was always a final play. There had to be.

"No." There was no menace in the words, only finality. "We've already taken you prisoner. If your superiors were to find out, any negotiations we made would be voided. Despite their assumptions, I've read the history of the UCP. They bill themselves as a benevolent, unifying organization, but really, they're as bad as their ancestors."

Pilsen's heart turned to lead. Only then did it become clear how well and truly LaVain had screwed him with his assignment. "W-well, that isn't entirely—"

Gabriel slammed a claw on the glass, cutting off further argument. "Beyond that, I don't trust you, Ambassador Pilsen. You have a busy and calculating mind, two things we have no need of here. Take solace that at least you have a beautiful place to spend the end of your life."

Pilsen could not have disagreed more. Oppressive gloom and spiderlike creatures did not make beauty. Still, he managed a smile.

"Even when you don't speak, you lie." Gabriel removed his claw from the glass. A small crack had formed from the impact. "Be seeing you."

"Wait!" The cover of Pilsen's container slid shut, returning him to the pitch black from which he had woken.

Chapter Nine

REVOLT

Huron oscillated between rage and fear. Gabriel's interaction with Pilsen had been mostly silent, but judging by the fear in the ambassador's eyes, it had not gone well. Pilsen's transport box was closed along with Crustacea's last opportunity to parley with the UCP. Only so much mistreatment could occur before Crustaceans would be considered terrorists in the eyes of organized government. Above, the last light of the sea dwindled to black. Huron tried not to think of the expeditions that had studied The Deep but failed. The results were the same every time: send something over the edge, it didn't come back.

"Your fear is natural," said Gabriel. "When I first saw the world's edge, it filled me with dread. We are born to look at it with dread."

Huron considered that the lights on the sides of the cart were a risk, a fast way to become prey in the darkness. She didn't need a scientist to understand that.

"Don't worry about the lights," Gabriel said.

"I don't like when you do that." Being taken prisoner was one thing. Losing her mind's privacy was another.

"Sorry." There was a hint of genuine contrition in Gabriel's voice. "Habits."

Huron pushed back the torrent of insults and jabs that would get her nowhere and instead found what remained of her diplomatic ability. "Why aren't you concerned about the lights?"

"There are many things that lurk in the depths below. While they might pose a threat to us, as with all things in life, something else poses a threat to them. On one of our deepest expeditions, our team came across a creature with orange lights running along its back, bigger than anything we had ever seen. So, when they returned, we ran a test. We put out several decoys covered in orange lights. Behold, unlike our previous probes, they weren't attacked."

"Clever." Huron listened intently enough to hear Gabriel's words while at the same time working her bindings. As with most egomaniacs, the lobster spoke of nothing but himself. They neared the end of the rail, where a makeshift platform was grafted to the side of a rock wall. Beside it, a lit tunnel led deeper into the rocks. That was where she would strike.

"So, you see, we are perfectly safe here. Now, if these lights were to suddenly turn white…well, that would be a different story."

Huron found the implied threat unnecessary; death surrounded them on all sides. Metal rods clicked below the cart as they pulled into the platform. "What do you have planned for Ambassador Pilsen?"

Gabriel let out a series of pensive clicks. "He must be made an example of. I know your intentions were good, Huron; we all do. But the UCP is nothing more than a gang of thieves. If we were to join their organization, we'd be back in cages before we saw any benefit."

The guard hoisted Huron out of the cart. "And what of the UCP's reprisal when they find their ambassador has been killed? Who is going to protect your people when they rain nuclear missiles from orbit?"

Annoyance flashed hot in Gabriel's voice. "There won't be any reprisal because the UCP doesn't—"

Huron took the moment to strike. Her claws were bound, but

she was still a warrior. She turned her body sideways, pulled her claws in, and shot forward with the edge of her shell. Surprise at the sudden assault was plain on Gabriel's face; he didn't have time to counter. Huron's shell grazed his forward antennae and hit him square in the mandible. Softer bits of shell cracked and broke. Gabriel tried to catch himself but slammed into the rock wall, sending up a cloud of debris.

Huron was readying a second charge when sudden, blinding pain shot up her side. Electricity arched through her body on a mad dash toward the ground. The world flashed different shades of white and yellow as spasmatic pain shook her. Her limbs shot out to the sides. Despite her best efforts, she fell to the ground; only then did Huron see the extended truncheon attached to the guard's claw. A fatal miscalculation.

Gabriel recovered, fussing over his mandibles with his front limbs. Bits of flesh and shell floated in a haze through the still water. When he spoke, it was with pure fury. "Oh, Huron. Here I was thinking you were starting to understand." He paused. "Hit her again, full voltage."

Huron didn't have the strength to flinch. When the electricity came, the world went black before she felt the pain.

Chapter Ten

BIG, METAL COFFIN

The excitement of donning a black market mech suit quickly faded as Zip descended into the darkness beyond Crustacea's continental shelf. Staring out at the abyss brought a swell of fear she couldn't hold back. It made her wish the metal abomination surrounding her had a cupholder somewhere. Still, function served over form during bug wars. The suit was a generation old and built in the bulky style still influenced by Old Earth military tech. It looked like a cross between an outdated tank and a Greek statue. Luckily, it was more graceful than either.

Zip glided through the water with little effort. The creators might have spared style, but they made up for it with ruthless efficiency. The craft was designed with two objectives: to survive and to destroy anything that threatened survival. Zip's cockpit was just large enough to give her arms a complete range of motion, which was necessary to operate the suit in manual mode. The rest of the space was occupied by armor plating and emergency repair systems. The mech's original joystick control system was disassembled and strapped to the hull. Zip preferred the finesse of a traditional haptic rig despite the user manual's recommendation. A panoramic glass canopy gave her an unobstructed view of an unfamiliar ocean.

With each passing second, the view mattered less and less. The last visible light rays soon disappeared, leaving nothing between her and the impenetrable darkness. She asked herself then why she continued to take such jobs. The answer was simple; drinks on the prime worlds were expensive, doubly so when she drank to forget.

Small servo motors whirred at her feet as Zip descended near an underwater cliff face. She stayed far enough away to be barely visible and close enough to find cover among the rocks if something attacked her.

"If Huron's tracker is still doing its job, you should be coming up on them in a few hundred feet." The shrimp's metallic voice sounded familiar from the suit's onboard speaker; virtual assistants were supposed to sound mechanical.

"Looks good from my end." A domed sonar screen beeped at steady intervals. Nothing showed on her scopes. "And I'm not seeing any of those monsters you were so keen to tell me about." The detail had been excruciating, enough to populate Zip's nightmares for years to come.

"There is a reason I told you to descend without running lights." There was almost a hint of sarcasm.

Zip had dimmed most of the lights in the cockpit. The shrimp's stories might have been overblown, but she wasn't taking any chances. She descended into pitch black, taking small comfort in the distant glow representing the edge of the shelf. Based on Huron's tracker, they were still within her suit's depth capabilities. If she went too deep, the suit was bound to implode; there were automatic ascension controls for situations like that, but naturally, she had turned them off. Zip had seen one too many pilots squashed against the hull of a destroyer from an automatic eject to trust the manufacturers.

"You should be nearing her position now. See anything? I do hope she's alright."

Zip squinted into the darkness. It was impossible to see much of anything beyond the dim outline of scaffolding along the underwater cliff. "I see something, but I'm not sure what I'm looking at." She flexed her fingers around a pair of triggers built into the haptic controls. A slight touch and whatever she was looking at would become at least fifty percent lead.

"I'm afraid we don't have much intel on what you're up against down there."

Zip sighed. Bad intel, lousy visibility, giant ugly monsters. When she returned to the city, she would have a whole round to herself to forget she had ever visited Crustacea. There were plenty of blue planets out there; why did it have to be this one? "I'm going to move in for a closer look." She felt at risk of being spotted. She imagined the monstrous weapons that might be awaiting her. The lobsters were clearly adept at combat. Her armor wouldn't last long if whatever they created could pierce crustacean shells.

The platforms grew clearer. Zip keyed a few controls and set the cockpit's glass to its highest magnification. The system found a hint of motion down the side of the rock wall and focused on it. Through the gloom, she could see the hulking forms of two lobsters lit by orange running lights. An enormous crab was bound to the lid of a slender gray box bobbing behind them. Zip punched a few more commands and ran a heat scan. It was hard to see much of anything at a distance, but the cold-blooded crustaceans made any heat signature stand out. The center of the box glowed a faint purple. "I think I've got eyes on Pilsen and Huron."

"Well, that's good news," said Tom.

"Yeah, I'm not so sure about that." Zip watched as the trio moved to the edge of a platform. They removed what she assumed was Huron and left her to sprawl in the darkness just beyond Zip's vision. Zip leaned forward as far as she could. "I can't see a—"

White lights burst into life from the darkness, turning the black ocean into a sea of tiny stars. Zip hit the suit's jets, backing away as fast as possible. "Shit, shit, shit." Instinctively, she turned sideways, putting the thickest armor between her and the enemy."

"Problem?" asked Tom.

"You could say that." The lights pulsed, and Zip waited between breaths for impact. None came. The ocean was silent. It blinked white and then fell to darkness. Zip held her breath and counted to ten. There were no torpedoes and no harpoons, only silence. "Maybe I overreacted."

"Perhaps they were preoccupied?"

"Preoccupied with what?" The sonar dome gave a single, loud chime. "Fuck me." Zip looked at the device and knew she would hate what she found. The sonar pinged again. A figure took up the bottom of the screen, pushing toward her from below. "Hey, Tom, I think I'm in trouble."

"Oh?"

Zip pushed the suit's thrusters and pointed herself toward the bottom of the ocean. Her fingers hovered over the triggers. At first, there was nothing but the alternating strobe of the platform's lights. Then, she saw it. A hulking behemoth rose from the depths. The sheer size was enough to let her know that she wasn't being paid enough. Light glinted off hundreds of thick, white teeth that lined a gaping maw. Several sets of eyes stared at her, milky and glistening in the twilight.

"Tom?"

"Yeah?"

"I hate your planet."

Chapter Eleven

BEHEMOTH

Pilsen had plenty of time to think. After his brief chat with the leader of the lobster rebellion, he liked his odds of survival even less. Still, he hoped for a miracle. From the darkness, he plotted his political return. He would tell tales of the brutality he faced on Crustacea and martial a force large enough to make the planet pay for its political crimes. The people loved a wartime politician. Nothing was better for one's career than people dying in a land close enough to mean something but far enough away for the bloodshed to be censored.

A sudden lurch broke Pilsen from his dream; the harsh, cold reality of his imprisonment slammed into his chest. He could feel his weight shifting slowly to his shoes; nice shoes meant to impress. Instead, they sat covered in muck at the bottom of a damp box at the bottom of a damp planet. Life had its own sense of humor.

The box lid slid open, revealing the gloomy ocean beyond. Gabriel stood silhouetted against it. "Hello again, Ambassador Pilsen."

From Pilsen's position, the creature looked even bigger than before. Pieces of its shell were missing or cracked. Pilsen projected as much strength as he could muster. "Have you reconsidered your planet's diplomatic future with the UCP?"

Gabriel shook his head. "No, no, I haven't."

"Right."

"But if it would please you to know, Huron fought valiantly to rescue you." Gabriel stepped aside and motioned a claw toward the incapacitated crab. She was barely standing, her black eyes looking around lazily, stunned. "It was a fool's errand, of course, but honorable, nonetheless. I'm beginning to understand why the populace likes her."

"An upstanding political servant." The people also loved politicians who died for a cause. But it was a shit way to get reelected.

"I suppose you see yourself as much of the same?"

"I do what's asked of me."

Gabriel nodded and bumped a switch on the side of the container. Cold water rose to meet Pilsen's feet. Terror found its way into his throat. Time was well and truly out.

"Relax, breathe. You're only equalizing. There would be no point in drowning you."

Pilsen let out a sigh of relief. "Mercy, after all?" He tried to keep his mind off the retribution the people of Crustacea would face.

"No, not mercy. She won't come after you if you're dead."

"She?"

"Deep breaths, Ambassador Pilsen." Gabriel backed away steadily. "If you hold it in, your lungs will explode. Trust me, that's far more painful."

"W-wait. You can't seriously be considering this. I am an appointed ambassador of the UCP! This is at least three steps past the line for war crimes!" Kidnapping a messenger alone was considered a war crime, but there was no point in telling the brutes that. Pilsen's mind raced, trying to find a way out. He wasn't sure how far up the surface was, but he was sure he couldn't make it without dying from pressure sickness.

It was then he realized Gabriel wasn't the one backing away. A thin line ran down a metal platform from Pilsen to the edge of the shelf. Strange rock chunks surrounded by ghostly white debris clung to the surface. The farther he moved, the harder it became to make the pieces out. He watched as the orange lights of relative safety faded to inky blackness.

A flash of white light appeared from nowhere and temporarily blinded him. Pilsen jerked in his box; the after-image burned in his eyes. The light flashed again. There was less pain this time, and he observed lines of bulbs at the edges of the platform. They flickered on and off rhythmically, casting long shadows through the murk. Each passing flash made it a little easier to observe his surroundings.

White spots hung in the air like lazy snowfall. The rocks that lined the platform were sharp and familiar. Water moved up to his ankles as Pilsen leaned closer to the glass to get a better look. He noticed beautiful, multicolored shells during these brief moments of illumination, alongside smatterings of claws and shells. It wasn't long before he realized he was traveling backward through a graveyard.

The container stopped and rotated to face the abyss. Water trickled past Pilsen's stomach, but he no longer felt the cold. Fear took over every emotion and sent his heart hammering in his chest. *This is not how I die.* There would be no one to benefit from his life insurance policy besides a few very exotic, very dead houseplants. All that pension wasted.

Then, a spark glinted in the darkness. Pilsen leaned forward and nearly touched the glass. It was a mech suit, hovering just at the edge of the light's reach. It looked old and bulky. He only knew one person that would have brought such machinery along. "Zip!" Pilsen pounded at the glass, trying to get her attention as water crept over his chest. The mech suit turned. "YES! Zip, I'm over here!" *I'll recommend her for a thousand commendations. She'll never have to work a grunt job like this again.*

The spark that had lit the flame of Pilsen's political ambitions was back. The future was bright. Brighter for him, of course, but there was still a hazy shine to Zip's, as well. She could be his driver. That was better than working in the ass end of the galaxy, right?

White light flashed, and Pilsen's joyous pounding ceased. A horrible creature composed of teeth and eyes rose from the deep as water reached Pilsen's lower lip. *Attack the big mech suit. Go for the big shiny thing.* The creature failed to respond in kind.

Milky white eyes set atop a barrel frame shot toward Pilsen at an alarming speed. A violent wake shook the container back and forth, but he hardly noticed. Water passed his nose; he held what little was left of his breath. The creature's jaws opened wide to reveal a yawning chasm of thick, pointed teeth.

I hope it's quick.

Around Pilsen, the sides of the box clicked and separated. He drifted upward, a result of the air in his lungs that made him buoyant. He floated away from the platform with no effort toward escape. This was the end, and it had been a wasted life.

Then, a sound interrupted his thoughts. A line of micro missiles erupted from the mech and streaked toward the creature. They hit with little effect. *Some things are just too big.* Years of school and political training, and here he was, about to die in the gullet of a giant fish on a crab planet. *There are some things in life you can't plan for.* The overwhelming mass of the creature loomed ahead and surrounded him, cutting off what little light remained. As the creature's mouth closed, a deep, guttural groan shook his body. Pilsen let out his last breath and sent bubbles floating toward nothingness. Blinding pain crushed him from every conceivable angle.

Then there was confusion. Then nothing.

Chapter Twelve

LAST DITCH EFFORTS

Huron woke with the distinct sense that she was lucky to be alive. Every muscle ached. It required extreme effort to move her limbs. She opened her eyes to an extended platform bathed in pulsing white illumination. Two lobsters stood silhouetted at its edge. A small box moved along the platform toward the darkness of the deep. She knew it was Pilsen, and her heart sank.

Memory arrived in flashes, then a steady stream. She remembered the crackling note of electricity that punctuated her last conscious moment. Adrenaline flooded her battered body. This was it. Fight or die.

The pain faded to numbness, a last-ditch effort at survival. *Fuck these lobsters.* Huron surprised even herself. It wasn't the first time she had cursed, but it wasn't typical. Far more shocking was the lack of attention from her captors. They didn't turn or even move; they just stared out at the black ocean in anticipation of some unknown thing.

Opportunity. Huron moved slowly, half out of caution, half because her balance was a thing of the past. Each step was sluggish and tender. Soon, a line of fire erupted out of the dark ocean and arched toward the depths underneath the platform. Tiny missiles shot out, leaving streaks of dark bubbles as the thrusters faded. Blooms of orange fire burst, illuminating a hulking form that rose from the deep like a great balloon made of teeth. Its milky eyes turned in every direction, twitching and rolling. Pilsen's container sprang open and left the poor human far beyond his natural depth. She was surprised the pressure didn't immediately crush him. *We are all doomed.*

The beast swallowed Pilsen in one lazy gulp as it ignored the hail of missiles on its backside. It took less than three seconds. Crustacea's hopes of joining the universal stage were lost. Huron felt a sinking feeling, followed by a near-instant upswell of rage. She found her footing and put her back against the rock wall. The outcroppings were sharp as she severed the bond around her right claw in one, clean motion. She clipped her left band and moved silently toward Gabriel and his guard.

The pair were entranced by the beast's display of power. Gabriel's elation was broadcast through the water like a psychic radio. "Look at the size, look at the magnificence. She is beautiful!"

Huron eyed the stun baton on the guard's right claw. *Not letting that happen again.* Just as the guard noticed, she moved and brought her claw to bear on its four right legs. With a mighty snap, she severed them in a single blow that sent the lobster crashing onto its side. Instinctively, the guard broke his fall with his claw but ignited the stun baton in the process. Electricity arched through the guard's underbelly, sending his limbs out and bringing him down atop the weapon. Huron backed away and watched as the creature jerked and trembled, unable to let go of the trigger. Bubbles of steam rose from beneath its shell as it cooked from the inside out.

"No!" shrieked Gabriel. "Huron, you fool!"

Huron backed up for another charge, but Gabriel was fast. He bore down on her with two massive claws that swept in from the sides. The right clipped her shell and nothing more, while the left punctured the soft flesh of her underside. It ripped and tore as white mist rose before her. The pain was immense and immediate but dulled by adrenaline; Huron tried to ignore that it was her own insides floating before her. "You've doomed us all!"

Gabriel recoiled. Huron lunged at his legs and snapped with her left claw. She felt it close around something, but Gabriel's retreat was quick. With his powerful tail, he shot backward and landed on his feet. "I am the next stage in our evolution, Huron. I will not die subservient to those who did us so much harm."

"There is more than one species in the ruling body of the galaxy, Gabriel." Huron was too tired to argue. She could see the behemoth gliding in the distant waters. Suddenly, the sputtering sparks of the baton, still slowly frying the guard, were too bright.

"You fear the creature. But what you should fear is me." Gabriel lunged forward, claws outstretched. Huron raised her own before her face and braced for impact. The ground was too smooth to absorb the force of Gabriel's blow. She slid backward and collided with the rock wall, where a jagged edge scraped along her shell.

Before she had a chance to recover, Gabriel dug in. Unimaginable pain lanced up her right side. A leg floated up in the water. Could it be her own? She couldn't tell anymore. Huron fell and felt fresh agony course through her body.

"There are worst places to die," said Gabriel. He put his claws between the joints of Huron's arms. She tried to break his grip, but it was too strong. "If it helps, know you'll be remembered as someone who fought for your people." Gabriel's claw snapped down and severed Huron's arm at the joint.

She barely felt it. Instead, a vague sense that she had made a critical mistake washed over her. "You—" She faltered. The words were coming from far away. A sudden current washed over them both, kicking up pieces of what had recently been Huron's body. *What is that? Death on the tide?* Huron stared into Gabriel's eyes and mustered the last of her strength. "You will go down as a radical that doomed your people."

Time slowed, and Huron watched death arrive. Gabriel's face contorted, angry, surprised, and in pain. This was the final moment. Then, his grip slackened as a metal blade drove through the front of his head; Huron was barely aware of the mech suit that followed.

The world faded to black. A face looked down at her from behind a domed glass window. She tried to call out to it, but everything was far too heavy. She needed to rest.

Chapter Thirteen

BIG FISH

ZIP FELT ABSOLUTE TERROR AND GUILTY RELIEF AS PILSEN WAS swallowed whole. The terror was obvious. She had seen unimaginable, horror-inducing creatures in her travels, but none of them ever made her feel so helpless.

Relief came in the form of limited options. There was no longer an ambassador to save. Her contract —what remained of it, anyway — consisted of getting back to the ship and getting the hell away from Crustacea.

"Zip, what is happening down there?"

And then, of course, there's the shrimp.

"Well, rescuing the ambassador is off the table. I'm heading back topside." She kicked the jets to begin her ascent.

"And what of Huron?"

I'm not getting paid to rescue Huron.

"She hasn't moved, Tom. I'm not sure she's still among the living."

"You have to at least check, please." The mechanical nature of Tom's voice made it hard to convey any real emotion, but Zip suspected he was pleading.

"I go down there, odds are I'm not coming back."

"I understand."

Zip's finger hovered over the ballast controls. One press and she'd be rocketing toward the surface, toward safety. *Stupid conscience.* She let out a growl. *It's going to get you killed.* She willed herself to press the button, to save herself. One simple press. "Do I need to remind you that my weapons had no effect on that thing?"

"I said I understand."

"A passive-aggressive shrimp. Who would have thought?"

"I assure you, I meant nothing other than—"

Zip stopped listening when bright sparks of electricity lit up the platform. A lobster convulsed on the ground where a crab's silhouette was illuminated by the stark light of a stun torch. "Your lucky day, Tom." The beast turned below, looking for more food; Pilsen wasn't more than an appetizer. "Huron's alive, and I'm going to get her."

"Oh, happy—"

Zip clicked the radio off. The last thing she needed during a fight was a distraction. She slowed her breath and shot forward. The white lights glinted off her suit's metal shell, turning it into an undersea beacon. *If the beast didn't want me before, it sure as hell wants me now.* Zip brushed the suit's triggers aside and grabbed the melee control stick. Missiles were preferable, but a small miss would leave Huron as mincemeat – lump crab – something unpleasant.

Back at the platform, Huron struggled with the remaining lobster. A cloud of white detritus formed around them. Odd chunks floated through the water. Zip pushed a toggle and extended a blade from the suit's right arm before increasing her speed. Lobster shells were tough, but nothing would stop a metal knife at forty miles an hour.

Braced for impact, Zip quickly ran through the next steps of the battle. *Opening: stab the big fucking lobster. Intermission: recover from hitting the rock wall at suicidal speed.* The suit could take it, but her body wouldn't be happy. *Finale: grab Huron, rocket to the surface.* As far as plans went, it wasn't the most complicated. But simple often won the day.

She finished her mental checklist and found the battle was deteriorating fast. Huron watched a claw float through the water as she was pinned by the giant lobster. A claw floated through the water. *Can crabs bleed out?* Had she known they were going to a bug planet, she would have done more research. With her sword arm in front of her, Zip rammed into the back of the lobster. She pushed the blade through what she hoped was its head.

The impact was immediate. Spiderwebs of pain fired through every bone in her body. Zip ignored the impact alarms and warning lights and reversed the suit's jets with her free hand. With the other, she lifted the lobster between her and the wall. The suit's servos whirred with effort but held amid the strain. Streams of bubbles erupted before her, making it impossible to see, but the sudden slowing of momentum was evident. The suit's feet ground against the platform, sending up ribbons of stripped metal and sparks. Zip tried to relax and make her body limp; the impact never came.

The bubbles cleared to reveal a very dead lobster skewered by her blade with a rock wall five feet ahead. *Small miracles. Intermission.* Zip flicked the blade forward and sent the lobster flying. It crashed into the wall with a muted thunk. Then, she turned toward Huron. The crab was clearly unconscious and dealing with the consequences of multiple severed limbs.

Long shot. Zip flicked a series of switches on the suit. Several small grapple cables shot out, which she attached via remote control to the unconscious crab. Upon finishing, the sound that left the world during battle came back. At first, only the quiet hiss of the suit's oxygen circulating through the cockpit was audible. But then she heard the steady beep of the sonar. *And you forgot about the giant fish.* Knowing exactly what she would see, Zip looked out at the ocean. Sure enough, the creature was turned around and headed straight toward them. The dead lobster sparked on the platform as bait. If Zip was a gambler, she wouldn't bet on the beast's finesse.

A strong current swept up the battle debris. Huron's body slid out from behind Zip and drew the tow cables taught. The behemoth's mouth opened wide and skimmed the platform's edge with its horror show of a maw; thick, jagged teeth lined in impossible numbers. Zip stood her ground, realizing what the finale of her one-woman show should be. "Usually, the things I play chicken with are a lot smaller than you." She hunched and braced her body to ensure the tow cables remained devoid of slack. *This is going to be tight.* The creature needed to be close enough that it couldn't turn to chase her but far enough away for the suit's jets to overpower the current.

She stared at the oncoming creature, taking in every detail. If she was going to die —which she wasn't— she wanted to take every last second from life. It had been a hard one, but there was always beauty in that which was worth doing. Rescuing Huron; that was worth doing.

The creature before her was hideous, the sheer magnitude awe-inspiring; interstellar battleships could fit in its gullet. The myriad milky eyes atop its broad, wrinkled head implied a long history of living in darkness. Zip wondered how many of its kind there were and what other creatures lurked in the far reaches of Crustacea's ocean.

A hundred feet or less. The current lifted the bait lobster off the ground and flung it against the rock wall. She wondered if Ambassador Pilsen had felt any pain in that gaping hellhole of a mouth.

Fifty feet. *Now or never.* Zip turned on every jet, booster, and means of propulsion the suit had. The elastic supports of the cockpit's haptic rig strained and pressed her back against the metal wall. The world outside became little more than a blue blur.

A mighty crash cut through the ocean's calm, followed by a deep rumble of collapsing rock. Bubbles and debris blocked the cockpit's viewport. Alarms blared, reminding Zip that she was not using the suit as its maker intended. *Whatever.* As long as rivets didn't pop off like champagne corks, they'd stay alive. A red readout informed the tow cables struggled but ultimately held. The force could rip Huron in half, but Zip had faith.

The world shook as she watched the depth gauge count down. Bubbles and debris cleared. Light blue silhouetted the black edge of the continental shelf, and she adjusted the boosters to aim far away from the unfathomable deep. Hesitantly, she checked the sonar screen. Several pieces of debris let out weak pings but indicated the behemoth wasn't following. They skimmed forward at immense speed, clearing the continental shelf in seconds. In the distance, Zip saw the twinkling lights of Crustacea.

"Holy shit." She let out her breath and flipped the radio switch. "Tom, I've got her. You need to get me a medical team and whatever the hell the Crustacean equivalent of a beer is."

Epilogue

ZIP SAT AGAINST THE PLUSH FABRIC OF HER CAPTAIN'S CHAIR AND cradled a bottle of distilled Crustacean liquor. She looked out at the setting sun. A day had passed since her journey to The Deep, and she awoke in a cold sweat every night as she remembered the horrors that lay there. Immediately after returning, she had gone to *The Hog's* medical bay and ran every conceivable scan. While the mech suit had held up, the pressurization hadn't been perfect.

Zip's body showed elevated levels of nitrogen. Luck, for once, was on her side. According to the scan, all she needed was a day's rest before space travel. A day spent checking *The Hog's* systems and coordinating Crustacean mechanics to patch the jagged holes in its belly. It sure as hell beat dying of an aneurysm at warp speed.

A small timer in the corner of the cockpit clicked over to zero and blurted a gentle alert. "About time." Zip keyed in a series of buttons and dials, her personal code to ensure no one could ever fly *The Hog* without her. Then, she turned on the shipboard comms. "You said you wanted to see takeoff, right? Well, you've got about five minutes." Zip looked over at the plastic sheet she had hastily taped to the co-pilot's chair and the bucket beneath it. She would say it was for queasiness, but in reality, *The Hog's* upholstery wasn't made to endure damp guests.

The cockpit door irised open, and Tom bounded toward the copilot's chair, a brick of fish flakes in one pincer and a metal translator in the other. His hydration apparatus dripped foul-smelling seawater onto the floor. "I do wish we could have waited for Huron to wake up."

Zip nodded. "Doctors say she's going to do fine, right?"

Tom nodded. "You're right." He fiddled with the chair's straps to get them around his body's odd proportions.

"Oh, don't bother with those." Zip indicated her own lack of a belt.

"But the safety restraints."

"Almost purely decorative. Anything that turns off the artificial gravity and pulls you out of that seat will pulp us long before a seat belt matters."

Tom's eyes twitched nervously. "This is a good idea," he reminded himself. The blaring volume of the translator made quiet pep talks impossible.

"Remember what we talked about?"

"Yes."

"Well, repeat it back to me then."

"We stand a better chance at a relationship with the UCP if we send back an ambassador of our own rather than an empty box meant to represent your corpse."

"Couldn't have said it better myself. Much smaller chance they nuke the planet from orbit when they meet you, Tom." Zip ran through her final pre-launch check, careful to keep an eye on Tom. There was a certain thrill that could only be found by watching someone's first exposure to space flight.

"Nuke us from orbit?! Is that really an option?! I thought—"

"Only kidding, Tom. You're going to have to get used to that."

"Right..." He fiddled with his abundance of limbs.

"The first ambassador from Crustacea, huh? What an honor." Before Tom could respond, Zip punched the engines, and they rocketed into the night sky.

THE END

59

About the Author

Ashton Macaulay is a fiction writer living in Seattle Washington. His other works include *The Nick Ventner Adventures,* tales of a drunken monster hunter traveling around the world in search of creatures that shouldn't exist.

Twitter: @RealMacAshton

Instagram: @Mac_Ashton

Website: MacAshton.com

Whiteout

Nick Ventner is a drunk with a blatant disregard for others. He's also damned good at hunting creatures that aren't supposed to exist. From amateur necromancers in the bayou to Sasquatch impersonators in the Pacific Northwest, Nick's seen it all. Even if some of the details might be a little fuzzy.

In *Whiteout*, Nick faces his greatest challenge to date. Accompanied by his trusty mountain guide, Lopsang, and his testy apprentice, James, Nick journeys into the Himalayas to settle a matter of pride and payouts, as he searches for the lost riches of Shangri-La rumored to lie within the mountain's peak.

However, the sudden arrival of Nick's greatest adversary, Manchester, complicates matters, and pits the two in a race towards the top, and both soon find that they have not just one another to contend with, but also a mythical and elusive yeti that has been terrorizing the mountain.

Featuring death-defying obstacles, hair-raising encounters with creatures from beyond, and a heavy dose of sarcasm along the way, Whiteout is sure to satisfy anyone looking for a fast-paced adventure novel brimming with action, suspense, and imagination. Not to mention the occasional whiskey on the rocks.

Aberrant Tales

Aberrant Tales is a collection unlike any other. Within this book are a variety of tales bursting at the seams with creativity and wonder. Tales of corporations that allow you to see into your own future. Tales of creatures that dwell within our dreams and nightmares. Tales of gallant knights battling through surreal, gothic landscapes to rescue the ones they love. These are stories that dare to be unique, to have a different point of view. Stories that entertain while conjuring up emotions of fear, excitement, and curiosity.

Aberrant Tales embraces a variety of narratives from the realms of science fiction, fantasy, and horror, and weaves them into one satisfying, eclectic package. Featuring twelve unique tales, *Aberrant Tales* will keep you on your toes as you experience the thrill of careening from one genre to another.

Aberrant Tales is proud to feature Ashton Macaulay's short science fiction/thriller *Future Solutions* among many fine others.

With *Aberrant Tales*, you truly never know what type of story you will encounter next. So prepare to fully immerse yourself in this collection of twelve fascinating tales filled with suspense, intrigue, and imagination. You'll find it to be one hell of a ride.